# Dinner with the Highbrows

Good Manners

## KIMBERLY WILLIS HOLT

### illustrated by KYRSTEN BROOKER

Christy Ottaviano Books

HENRY HOLT AND COMPANY ● NEW YORK

**B**ernard could hardly wait until next Saturday. He was invited to eat dinner with Gilbert Highbrow's family. Bernard had never eaten at a friend's house. He wondered if Mrs. Highbrow would cook pot roast, carrots, and rolls like his mom. Or maybe Mr. Highbrow would grill hamburgers in the backyard like his dad.

When the invitation arrived, Bernard's mom, Mrs. Worrywart, said, "The Highbrows live in such a fine house. They're sure to expect only the best manners."

Mr. Gilbert Highbrow requests the pleasure of your company for dinner Saturday 6:00 p.m.

R.S.V.P.

Mr. Bernard Worrywart
39 Cherry Lane

Special

All week Bernard's mom coached him.

At dinner on Monday, she said, "Remember, tell
Mrs. Highbrow how lovely the table is set.

"Place the napkin in your lap.

"And bow your head when they say the blessing."

Tuesday, Bernard practiced. *I'll remember,* he thought.

Then Wednesday his mother said, "Don't forget, no elbows on the table. Don't talk with food in your mouth. And for goodness' sakes, don't sing." Bernard tried to keep all the manners inside his head, but his mother wasn't through yet.

Thursday she added to her list. "Use the napkin to wipe your mouth. When you're finished, mention to Mrs. Highbrow how delicious the meal was. Then clear the table and offer to help wash the dishes."

On Friday, Bernard's mom said, "Most important, at the end of the meal, thank Mr. and Mrs. Highbrow for inviting you to dinner."

Eating dinner at the Highbrows' wasn't going to be easy.

Finally Saturday arrived. Bernard's mom drove him to the Highbrows' big fancy house.

As she turned past the iron gate and down the long driveway, she said, "Remember."

"I'll remember," said Bernard, trying to recall all the manners his mom had taught him.

After Bernard walked to the door, she added, "Don't forget to have fun!" Bernard held his breath and rapped on the door.

The Highbrows' butler opened the door.

"Mr. Bernard Worrywart, I presume?"

Bernard swallowed and squeaked. "Yes, sir."

"A Mr. Bernard Worrywart," the butler called out.

Bernard's palms felt sweaty.

"Welcome!" Mrs. Highbrow told Bernard. She waved good-bye to Bernard's mom.

"Hey, there, Bernie!" said Mr. Highbrow.

Gilbert slid down the staircase banister. "Hoorah! Bernard is here!"

"Hi," said Bernard.

Before Bernard could take one step inside the house, Mr. Highbrow grabbed his hat and shouted,

## "TIME FOR DINNER!"

The other Highbrow children, Billy, Logan, and Little Melly, raced out the front door, zoomed past Bernard, and piled into the family's chauffeur-driven limousine.

Gilbert grabbed Bernard's collar.

**"Come on! I'm hungry!"**

They slipped into the limo.

Little Melly poked Bernard's arm. **"I'm going to order first!"**

They drove until they reached Antonio's Italian Restaurant.

Inside, Bernard and the Highbrows sat at a round table covered with a white tablecloth.

Bernard got so excited he almost forgot all that his mother had said. Then he remembered.

"What a lovely table," Bernard told Mrs. Highbrow.

Mrs. Highbrow studied the table. "Why, yes, it surely is."

The waiter started to hand out the menus, but Mr. Highbrow held up his palm. "No need for those. We'll take the usual."

"Of course," said the waiter. A few minutes later, he returned with a huge platter of spaghetti and meatballs.

The Highbrows grabbed their forks. Bernard
pressed his hands together. Suddenly Little Melly said,
"Don't forget the blessing."
"Heavens to Betsy," said Mrs. Highbrow, "how could we forget?"
Bernard bowed his head.
Together the Highbrows said,

"Good grub. Good meat. Good gosh. Let's eat!
Amen!"

Bernard unfolded the napkin and placed it in his lap.
The Highbrows did not.

Bernard was careful to keep
his elbows off the table.
The Highbrows were not.

With lips pressed together, Bernard chewed
his spaghetti.

Mrs. Highbrow stuck a whole meatball in
her mouth and asked, "Bernard, does your family
ever eat here?"

Bernard swallowed, then wiped his mouth with
the napkin, and answered, "No, ma'am."

A trickle of sauce dribbled down Mr. Highbrow's chin. He swiped it with his sleeve. Then he **BURPED!**

The Highbrow children laughed. "Good appetite," Gilbert said.

Little Melly plucked a meatball off Bernard's plate.
The meatball slipped from her fingers,
rolled across the table, landed on the floor,
and crumbled.

"Ooops!"

Little Melly giggled.

"That reminds me of a song!" Billy yelled. He began to sing.
"On top of spaghetti . . . all covered with cheese . . ."
The rest of the Highbrows joined in.
"I lost my poor meatball when somebody sneezed . . ."
Everyone sang except for Bernard, who was trying
to remember everything his mother had told him.

Soon the spaghetti and meatballs disappeared into everyone's belly. Mr. Highbrow loosened his belt and leaned back.

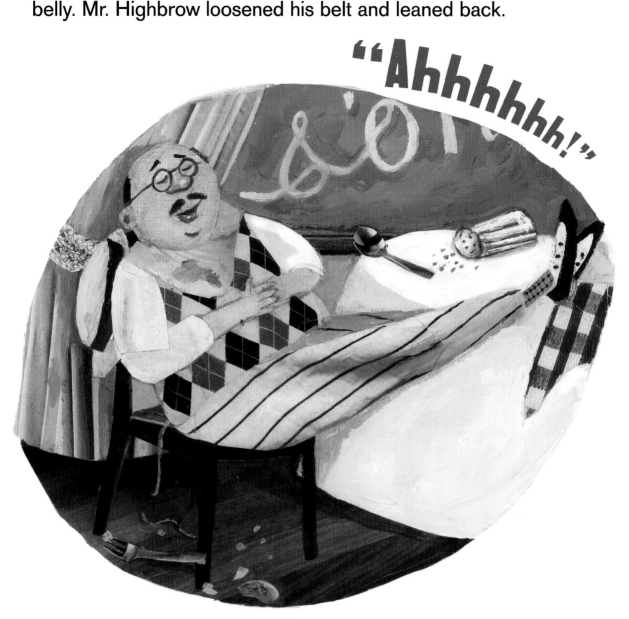

"Ahhhhh!"

"That was a delicious meal," Bernard said to Gilbert's mom.

Mrs. Highbrow picked at a speck of bell pepper between her teeth. "Yes, it surely was!"

"May I please be excused?" Bernard asked.

"Of course, dear," said Mrs. Highbrow.

Everyone looked confused when Bernard stood and stacked all their plates, then disappeared behind the swinging door.

"What a peculiar boy!" said Mrs. Highbrow.

In the kitchen, Bernard asked the dishwasher,
"May I help, please?"
"Sure," said the dishwasher who wasn't used
to such an offer.

Bernard washed the plates. He washed
the glasses. He washed the pots and pans, too.
When he was finished, he turned to discover every
single Highbrow peeking through the kitchen window.

Bernard knew he had forgotten something.
Something very important that his mother had taught
him. He thought very hard. Then he remembered.
"Thank you for asking me to dinner. I had a lovely time."

"You're welcome, dear," said Mrs. Highbrow.

Mr. Highbrow slapped Bernard on the back.
"Any time, Bernie."

"It's not over yet," said Gilbert.

"It's not?" Bernard asked.

"Of course not," the Highbrows said.

No talking with your mouth full

Say a blessing

Wash your hands before you eat

Don't reach across the table

Use your napkin

Say thank you

Elbows off the table

Eat your vegetables

To the memory of Bernard Waber,
who gave the world a crocodile named Lyle
—K. W. H.


For Nicholas and Kieran
—K. B.

Henry Holt and Company, LLC
*Publishers since 1866*
175 Fifth Avenue
New York, New York 10010
mackids.com

Library of Congress Cataloging-in-Publication Data
Holt, Kimberly Willis.
Dinner with the Highbrows / Kimberly Willis Holt ; illustrated by Kyrsten Brooker. — First edition.
pages   cm
Summary: The first time a friend invites Bernard to dinner, his mother gives him a long list
of rules to follow, such as keeping his elbows off the table and not speaking with his mouth full,
but he soon sees that being well-to-do does not mean one has the best manners.
ISBN 978-0-8050-8088-9 (hardback)
[1. Etiquette—Fiction.  2. Dinners and dining—Fiction.  3. Humorous stories.]  I. Title.
PZ7.H74023Din 2014   [E]—dc23   2013021125

Henry Holt books may be purchased for business or promotional use. For information
on bulk purchases, please contact Macmillan Corporate and Premium Sales Department
at (800) 221-7945 x5442 or by e-mail at specialmarkets@macmillan.com.

First Edition—2014 / Designed by April Ward
The artist used oil paint and cut paper on gessoed watercolor
paper to create the illustrations for this book.

Printed in China by Macmillan Production Asia Ltd., Kowloon Bay, Hong Kong (vendor code: 10).
1  3  5  7  9  10  8  6  4  2